Smoke
and
Shadow

Dragon Riders of Osnen Book 9

RICHARD FIERCE

Dragonfire Press

Cover design by germancreative.

Cover art by Rosauro Ugang

ISBN: 978-1-947329-66-9

CONTENTS

1

Darkness surrounded us, thick and impenetrable.

The torches that Domori and Haruna wielded helped a little, but the shadows seemed to slowly close in, suffocating the light. We stood in what appeared to be a small antechamber, which was ringed with pillars of stone, all of them crumbling with age.

"That doesn't look good," I whispered.

"No, it does not," Katori agreed.

I can't fit through the doorway. Sion's voice filled my mind.

I turned around and walked back to her, retrieving the collar and a robe from her saddle. I slipped the collar around her neck and waited as her massive body transformed into a human. She took the robe and covered her nakedness, then we joined Katori. She was holding her torch up to one of the pillars.

Despite the derelict appearance of the stonework, it was obvious that they had once been magnificent pieces of art. Here and there, lines in the stone revealed intricate patterns that had been lost to time.

"Were the people who built this place dragon riders?" I asked.

"No," Katori answered. "They were worshippers of *Ho-musubi*. If the legends are true, they were not good people. I suspect that is why the enenra was created. The victim was probably a sacrifice."

I couldn't imagine people doing something so horrid to one another. It was unconscionable. Katori moved away from the pillar, and I stayed close to her side. Since dragons had such amazing eyesight, I wasn't worried about Sion being outside of the torchlight.

Do you sense anything now that the wards are down?

I smell magic, Sion said. *Lots of magic.*

Good. The more items we can collect, the better.

"Sion says there is a great deal of magic down here. Should we let her lead the way?"

"Yes, but she must use caution. We don't know where the enenra is, and I would rather not run into it ill-prepared."

I am not afraid of this enenra creature, Sion said. *Yet I will do as Katori asks.*

"Haruna, you will stay here and guard the doors. Unless it is one of us, do not let anything pass by you. Shut the doors, if you must." Katori pulled the pendant from around her neck and handed it to him.

The Curate accepted it and offered a bow.

"Come," Katori said. "Let us be quick. This place gives me a bad feeling in my stomach."

Sion took the lead and disappeared among the shadows. I walked with Katori, and Domori followed behind us. The light of their torches illuminated a small area around us, but the gloom seemed to snuff the light from existence. I peered ahead, trying to see Sion. I could hear her footsteps, but the light didn't stretch far enough to glimpse her.

Slow down, I told her. *I can't see you.*

I'm not moving fast, she replied. *I'm barely a few feet in front of you. This darkness is unnatural.*

Is it caused by magic?

Yes, though I don't know why anyone would want perpetual darkness.

The antechamber had three doorways, all of which were missing the doors. We went through the center one, an arched entrance that took us into a short hall. The walls were covered with cobwebs, and some hung down from the ceiling. I shivered several times when my hand and face inadvertently touched their silky strands.

At the end of the hall, we entered another doorway. Sconces were affixed to the walls beside the entrance, and Katori lit them with her torch. The darkness was pushed back and revealed what appeared to be a prayer garden. The floor was covered with smooth river stones arranged in a swirling pattern, and two large statues of armored men stood guard from either side of the room. Their armor resembled Domori's, with the faces of the statues also covered with demonic masks.

"There's an inscription," Katori said, drawing my attention to where she was looking. Set against the far wall was a large stone that had a flowing script engraved upon its surface.

"What does it say?"

"'Here in silence you will find the flames.'"

"What does that mean?" I asked.

"I don't know. Perhaps it is a reference to the god of fire."

"There's something over here, too," Domori said.

He was on the opposite side of the room. Katori and I joined him, and I saw what he was talking about. A small pool of clear liquid sat within the depression of a square stone, but the liquid flowed out in thin trickles along what appeared to be a miniature version of a waterway.

"It looks like water," I said as I reached down to dip my fingers in it. Katori's hand snatched my wrist aside, startling me. I looked at her and she shook her head.

"That is not water. At least, not natural water. It flows away from the pool of its own accord."

I knelt in front of the stone and looked closer. She was right. The liquid moved up the stone, away from the depression.

"It must be directed by magic," I said.

"Yes, but where does it go?" Katori asked.

She brought the torch closer to the stone and followed one of the trickles. It flowed along the waterway and disappeared under the wall. The torch flickered as if moved by an unseen breeze and the liquid caught fire. The flames raced across the surface of the stone and the entire room lit up.

"That's definitely not water," I muttered.

Whatever it was, it was flammable. And it saturated the walls, though they didn't erupt in flames as the trickles did. The magic in this place was odd. Sion leaned down and sniffed the burning liquid.

"It is not water," she confirmed through trembling lips. "It is dragon saliva."

"Dragon saliva is flammable?"

"How do you think we breathe fire?" she asked.

"I don't know. I assumed it was by magic."

"Not everything is magic."

"Since when did you learn to speak in your human form?" I asked.

Sion smiled but didn't reply.

"She is correct," Katori said. "In the mouth of a dragon, there are two sacks located on either side of the upper jaw. When they excrete the liquid contained within them and it touches their saliva, it creates a chemical reaction that makes fire."

"Truly?"

"Truly."

Perhaps I'd missed that in my studies. Or perhaps I had read that and simply forgotten it. Either way, I was surprised. I'd always assumed that a dragon's ability to breathe fire was powered by their magic. Especially since some dragons had more than one breath weapon.

Sion looked to the doorway across the room and her brow furrowed. "There's magic in there," she said. "I can feel it."

"So can I," Katori muttered. "I feel it thrumming in my veins. It must be a powerful trinket."

"Then let's go find it," I said.

I strode through the doorway and entered the room. The walls glowed with the same light as the prayer garden, and it became apparent that the entire temple must be illuminated by the strange light. I didn't see anything that looked like a magical item to me. There was an altar with a golden bowl atop it, and along the far wall was a table covered with dried sheaves of some kind of plant.

"Incense," Katori said, nodding toward the table.

"Is that what's humming with magic?" I asked.

"No. It's that." Katori pointed to the bowl.

Sion walked over to the altar and examined the bowl, but she didn't pick it up.

"It has powerful enchantments woven into it,"

she said. "Though I do not know what they do. The magic is different from anything I've seen before."

"The spells are confusing," Katori chimed in. "They seem to contradict each other, yet they flow in harmony. It is a mystery."

"Well, it's a good thing we don't need to know what they do," I said. "We just need the magic to power a different spell."

A cloth bag was on the table, full of the incense sheaves. I picked it up and dumped the contents onto the table, then grabbed the bowl and put it inside the bag. Katori stared at me in silence for a moment.

"This feels wrong," she said.

"I'm sure it does, but it's the only way to free Maren and restore magic." I paused. "Please don't back out on me."

We stared at each other in silence, and Katori finally nodded.

"I will keep my word, but that doesn't mean I have to like what we are doing."

"Fair enough," I replied as I slung the sack over my shoulder. "Do you sense anything else?"

Sion nodded. "Yes. It's coming from the altar, but the altar itself is not the source."

"It's inside the altar," Katori said. "Clever."

"How do we get it out?"

Katori nodded at Domori. The man drew his

blade and spun around, striking the front of the altar with his sword. The façade cracked, revealing a hidden compartment. Katori removed the broken pieces and reached into the partition. She struggled for a moment, then pulled her arm free. Gripped in her hand was a scepter.

"It's heavy," Katori said.

"And powerful," Sion added.

"Yes, the magic is making my arm tingle. Open the bag."

I did as Katori asked and she dropped the scepter in with the bowl.

"If our luck continues like this, we'll—"

An ominous sound echoed off the walls, cutting off my words. We all exchanged looks, and the noise faded.

"What was that?" I whispered.

"A cry of death," Katori answered.

2

"What do you mean?" I asked.

"I don't think we're alone down here."

"Did someone follow us?"

"That isn't likely. It must be the enenra. It's probably wailing to itself."

Katori tilted her head and listened, but there was only silence now. We waited a moment longer, but the stillness remained.

"Let us continue," Katori said. "I want to leave this place."

I looked at Sion. "Anything else?"

"Not in here," she replied. Sion closed her eyes and sniffed the air. "This way."

She walked over to the table of incense and paused.

"What is it?" I asked.

"There's a door here," she replied.

I didn't see one. There was only a solid wall behind the table. I looked at Katori, who shrugged.

"I can't feel any magic except for those things in the bag. Sion, do you know how to break illusions?"

"No."

"Let me try to help you, then. Picture the door you sense to be there within your mind. Then push against it with your willpower. Use as much force as you need to."

I watched the wall and must have been subconsciously holding my breath. My lungs started burning, and I exhaled as Sion broke the enchantment. The wall rippled like water, and then a wooden door became visible.

"You learn quickly," Katori complimented.

"It wasn't difficult," Sion replied. "Thank you for your help."

"Aside from wanting to hide something, why else would someone use an illusion to hide a door?" I asked.

"To keep others from opening it," Katori replied.

A chill ran down my back, but I wasn't sure why. I wasn't afraid. At least, I didn't think I was. I'd faced a dracolich, a necromancer, a basilisk, and the wrath of the Assembly. Potentially facing an enenra, whatever that truly was, seemed inconsequential in comparison.

I pushed away my doubts and walked past Sion, grabbing onto the door handle. It didn't budge.

"It's locked," I said.

Domori motioned with his hand. "Move aside."

We cleared the way and Domori sheathed his blade, then took a few steps back before sprinting ahead. He lowered his shoulder and collided roughly with the door. There was a loud crash, but the door held firm. Domori staggered back and grunted.

"It didn't give at all," he said.

Katori knelt before the door and eyed the keyhole.

"I can pick the lock, but it's going to take me some time. If the lock is rusted, it will be even more difficult to unlock it without breaking something."

"There's something back the way we came," Sion said. "I didn't notice it before, but I smell it now."

"I don't like the idea of splitting up, but maybe we should," I suggested. "Sion and I will go see what's back there, and you two can stay here and work on getting the door open."

Katori looked at me. I could tell by her expression that she didn't like it any more than I did, but she nodded.

"If we can get the door open, we'll wait for you to return before going in."

"We'll be back as soon as we find what Sion senses. If not …"

"If you are gone too long, Domori and I will come searching for you."

I nodded. "Can I take one of the torches?"

"Take mine." Domori offered his.

"Now go," Katori said. "And be quick."

Sion and I backtracked the way we'd come. We passed through the prayer garden and into the hall, then turned right, down another corridor. With the walls glowing from the light of dragon saliva, it seemed I had no need for the torch. The corridor ended, opening up into a massive empty room.

"Where is the magic coming from?" I asked.

"There," Sion replied, pointing to a set of bronze double doors.

They were similar in appearance to the ones at the main entrance, but these didn't have anything engraved on them. They were plain and smooth, the only 'decoration' being a large hook on each door that held a thick wooden block in place.

"That looks like it's meant to keep something in," I said.

"The magic is coming from inside. We can leave it behind."

I set the cloth sack down on the floor and considered our options.

"Maren said it would take an immense amount of magic to create a bridge to the island," I said. "We need everything we can get our hands on."

Sion stepped over to the door and easily lifted the wooden block, setting it against the wall. She pulled one of the doors open and peered inside.

"It looks safe."

Knowing she wouldn't put me in danger, I

followed her as she entered the room. Except, it wasn't a room. It was a vaulted cavern. Stalactites and stalagmites were everywhere, all in varying sizes and shapes, and I could hear water dripping in several locations. Unlike the rest of the temple, the walls of the cavern weren't glowing. Good thing I'd taken one of the torches. I walked beside Sion and shined the torch around, but there wasn't much to see.

"Are you sure there's magic in here?"

"Yes," Sion said. "It's all around us."

"Where's the source, though? I don't see any—"

And then I spotted something. It reflected the torchlight and I could tell it was made of metal.

"That's the source," Sion said.

I approached cautiously and rested my right hand on the hilt of my sword. I had an odd feeling about the cavern, but there was nothing to indicate anything out of the ordinary.

"Careful," Sion said. "The magic is doing something."

I paused mid-step. "Is it a trap?"

"No." She hesitated. "I don't think so."

She sounded less than confident. I took a step. Then another. And another, until I was standing before the metal object, which I realized was an enormous brazier. A thick pile of ashes filled the bottom of it.

"Is the brazier the source of the magic?"

Sion growled lowly. "No. It's in it."

I set the torch on the edge of the brazier and drew my sword. Perhaps the item was buried under the ash. I jabbed the blade into the ashes and pushed it around. There was a scraping sound as the tip slid across the bottom, but I didn't feel anything. The brazier was roughly six feet across, and my sword didn't reach far enough to sift through the rest of the ashes.

"Climb in," Sion said.

"I'm going to. I just don't want to get ash all over me."

With a sigh, I climbed into the brazier and immediately regretted it. My boots sunk into the ash pile, covering them with filth. I picked the torch up and held it out with my left hand and moved my sword with the other. Something solid connected with my blade.

"I think I found it."

I maneuvered my blade until I had leverage against the thing, then I pushed down, forcing it up through the ashes. It wasn't heavy, but holding the torch and only having my mangled arm to use made it awkward. After a few failed attempts, I was finally able to get the thing up enough that I could partially see it.

"What is it?" Sion asked.

"I'm not sure."

I set my sword aside and grabbed onto whatever

was poking up through the ash, then lifted it. Horrified, I dropped it and staggered back, almost tripping.

"It's a ribcage!" I hissed. "A *human* ribcage!"

Snatching my sword up, I hurriedly climbed out of the brazier and stomped my feet to get the ash off.

"This is disgusting."

I sheathed my blade and brushed off the ash that refused to come free from stomping, then held my hand away from the rest of my body. There was no way for me to be sure, but I feared the ash was human remains.

"I think the sewer in Tiradale was worse," Sion replied. "You smelled of that place for days."

"I did?"

"Yes."

"Why didn't you tell me?"

"Humans are gross, and you often stink. I thought you knew."

I laughed despite my disgust. Sion watched me, a smile on her lips.

"It's not the bones, is it?" I asked. "Please tell me that's not the source of the magic."

"They are," Sion confirmed. "They are not something we can use, however. The magic radiating from them isn't from spells or enchantments."

"So I climbed in there for nothing?"

"Yes."

I snorted and shook my head, looking back at the ribcage that now rested at the top of the ashes.

"Katori said that an enenra is created when a person is burned to death. Do you suppose those bones belong to the person that became one?"

"It is probable," Sion said. "With how the magic is acting around them, I think that person may have been the sacrifice."

I shuddered. "Let's get back to Katori. Maybe they managed to get the door unlocked."

A creaking sound echoed off the cavern walls, followed by the door we entered through slamming shut. I looked at Sion, but she ignored me and sniffed the air.

"What is it?"

Sion growled, her eyes scanning the cavern. The sound wasn't anywhere near as imposing as when she was in dragon form. The flames of the torch flickered, and noise from the brazier caught my attention. Just as I turned to look, the flames leaped from the torch and into the brazier, and the cavern was plunged into darkness.

3

"Sion?"

"I'm here."

Her hand touched my arm. I looked around, but there was no light at all, not even from the doors at the entrance. The sound of dripping water rang out, the only noise in the cavern aside from my breathing. And Sion's, though hers was quieter than mine.

"We need to get out of here," I said. "Can you lead me? I can't see anything."

Sion took my hand and I blindly followed her. She stepped slowly, making it easy for me. I could feel the closeness of the stalagmites, their bulky forms looming in the darkness around me. Sion stopped.

"We are at the doors," she said.

I pressed my hands against the smooth metal surface and pushed, but the door didn't move.

"Help me push."

"I am."

That gave me pause. If Sion's strength alone wasn't enough, then mine added to it would make no difference.

"Can your fire melt bronze?" I asked.

"Yes, but these doors are warded. My flames will do nothing against them."

"Then how do we get out?"

Suddenly, the darkness lifted.

I turned around. Black and red paper lanterns hung from the stalactites, illuminating the cavern. In front of the brazier, people stood in two rows, lining the walkway to it. They wore white robes with cowls over their heads, and they remained silent.

The doors behind me opened. I tried to go through them before I realized it was an illusion. My eyes deceived me, but my sense of touch did not. The cold metal of the doors hadn't moved at all. And then I noticed Sion was gone.

"Sion?" I looked around.

Can you hear me? Her voice came through the bond.

Yes. Where are you?

I am here beside you.

I don't see you.

The illusion hides me, but I am here. Nothing you see is real. It is but a moment in time, replayed by magic.

I looked back at the robed people. They may not be real, but they certainly seemed so. Everything I was seeing looked real.

"Bring him."

At the doors stood an imposing man. He was

tall, taller than me by a foot, though not as big as Hrodin. His hair was short, gray as ash, and sleeked back. A kempt goatee framed his jaw, and his eyes were a piercing blue. He wore robes of green silk trimmed in gold, and a small wingless dragon was sewn into the material along his right sleeve.

Behind him, two men in white robes held a third man between them. His arms were bound with rope and fear shone in his eyes.

"Please, my lord! I beg you! Don't do this."

"Your pleas do not honor *Ho-musubi.* He requires strength and loyalty. Are you not loyal to the flame, Kashima?"

The bound man, Kashima, swallowed hard and nodded.

"I am loyal, my lord Shirasaki … but my family …"

"Will be honored by your sacrifice," Shirasaki said. "Take him to the altar."

The two men forcefully escorted Kashima through the cavern to the brazier. They untied his hands, then wrapped the ropes around hooks that stuck out from the sides of the brazier. The man struggled to free himself, but all he did was cause the ropes to cut his wrists. Thin trails of blood dripped down into the brazier.

Shirasaki walked through me, though I didn't feel anything, and slowly made his way to where the people were gathered. I followed after him, marveling at the realism of the illusion. His robes rustled, his hair moved, and the whispered prayers of his followers sent chills down my back.

What I'm seeing actually happened in the past? I asked Sion.

Yes. I don't know why, but the magic has recreated this moment.

Maybe there's something we're supposed to witness?

Maybe.

Shirasaki reached the brazier and turned to face the crowd. His gaze seemed to fall upon me, though I knew that was impossible. Still, it was unsettling.

"Faithful of *Ho-musubi!*" His voice echoed loudly off the walls. "As the Holy Book tells us, we must make a sacrifice to the flames during the full moon. Kashima volunteered his life, but now he struggles to remain faithful to his oath. Let us pray that his commitment is strengthened."

A chorus of voices rose in a steady chant, but the words were in a different language. They stretched out their hands toward the brazier, repeating the same phrase over and over.

These people are insane, I said.

They are zealots, I think. Nothing here seems normal.

"Please release me," Kashima begged. "I don't want to die."

"Life is found in the fire," Shirasaki said. "Though your faith is weak, *Ho-musubi* accepts your sacrifice."

"Please, no!"

Shirasaki ignored the man's pleas and raised a hand, chanting something that sounded more like magic than another language. A ball of orange flame formed in Shirasaki's hand, and I could feel the heat from where I stood. He hurled the ball at Kashima's feet and the brazier erupted in flames. The crowd continued their prayer, all of them chanting in unison.

Kashima screamed.

I was horrified, but no matter how hard I tried, I couldn't turn my eyes away from the gruesome sight. The fire burned Kashima from his feet up, the flames licking at his clothes and burning his flesh. His screams were the worst part, and I feared I would never be able to forget them.

"He is purified by the flames," Shirasaki said loudly, raising his voice to be heard over the screaming. "Let us usher his soul to *Ho-musubi!*"

Kashima fell to his knees, fully engulfed. He issued a garbled cry, and then his body turned to ash and collapsed. Shirasaki's expression changed briefly to confusion, but he shook his head and joined in the prayer with his followers.

It was a horrible thing to witness. I could feel bile rising into my throat and thought for sure I would be sick. Smoke rose from the ashes, but there was something unnatural about it. The color was off, and the tendrils rose to the cavern's ceiling, coalescing into a large cloud. The crowd began to point and whisper among themselves, ceasing their prayers. Shirasaki ignored them.

The cloud of smoke began to swirl, forming into the shape of a terrifying visage. It appeared to be a creature of some sort, with glowing cerulean eyes. Claws formed, along with a gaping maw. Fear surged through me and I almost turned to run, but Sion reminded me that it was an illusion.

It looks real, I said.

Appearances can be deceiving.

The creature of smoke, or the enenra as Katori had called it, swooped down and began slaughtering the white-robed people. They tried to flee, but the doors slammed shut and people on the other side were shouting about a curse. There was nowhere for the people to escape, and the enenra easily cut through their ranks.

Some people died from its claws slicing their bodies in half. Others were snatched up in its jaws. Through it all, Shirasaki watched helplessly. The two men who'd escorted Kashima to the brazier drew their swords and foolishly tried to attack the enenra. Their blades passed through the creature, doing no harm at all. The enenra lashed out at one of them, flaying the man with its claws. The other man was slammed into a stalagmite. He went unconscious, and the enenra lifted his still form and impaled him on the jagged rock formation.

I kept telling myself that it wasn't real, that it had happened long ago and wasn't happening right before my eyes. And yet, it was real. Real in the sense that it was an actual event, and I had witnessed the creation of the enenra. Katori's master had been right. The creature did exist, and it was a force of vengeance, unlike anything I'd ever seen before.

It slaughtered everyone until only Shirasaki was left. The man knelt and prayed, begging to be spared. The enenra hovered around him, a gleeful expression on its smokey face.

"There is no life in the flames," it said, its voice a haunting sound. "There is only death."

The enenra picked Shirasaki up and tossed him into the brazier, the flames hungrily devouring him. The man screamed just as Kashima had, and I felt a disturbing sense of justice in the act. His screams eventually stopped and he died, burned by the very flames he'd conjured. The enenra snaked through the air to the doors, but it couldn't force them open or slip underneath them.

It began to wail, its cries echoing eerily throughout the cavern. The illusion slowly faded, forcing the darkness to return to the cavern. My heart was pounding in my ears, and I was clenching the hilt of my sword tightly.

"It's over," Sion said. "The vision has ended."

"That was horrible," I replied.

"Yes, it was."

The brazier erupted with flames, along with the torches on the walls, driving the darkness back.

Tendrils of smoke rose from the ash, forming into a cloud just like they had in the vision. I tossed the useless torch down, turned, and ran.

4

"We need to get the doors open!"

Sion and I ran through the cave back to the bronze doors. I threw myself bodily against them, but the only thing it resulted in was pain lancing through my shoulder. I hissed in a breath and looked to where the enenra was. The smoke was still forming into a cloud.

"Take this collar off," Sion said. "The doors are warded, but I'll try to flame them."

I did as she asked and unlatched it from around her neck, placing it onto my belt, then stepped away as her body elongated and shifted back into her dragon form, ripping the robe to shreds. She opened her jaws and breathed fire at the doors. I ducked behind a large stalagmite to avoid the heat, peering out after the flames died. The doors were undamaged.

Sion growled and clawed at them. Her powerful talons left thick scratch marks, but otherwise, the doors held firm. She turned and whipped her tail into them, roaring in rage. Her tail did less damage than her claws.

"There's got to be another way out of here," I said, stepping out from behind the stalagmite. I looked toward the back end of the cavern. No torches were there, and the darkness felt more ominous now.

I don't see one, Sion replied.

I'd almost forgotten that she couldn't speak audibly in dragon form and it startled me.

Do you sense any wards over there? Perhaps there's another door, one easier to break through?

I don't sense anything, she said. *You should hide. I'll fight the enenra.*

How will you do that? It's made of smoke.

Nothing is stronger than a dragon.

I didn't doubt that, but strength was an entirely different factor here.

I think we should check anyway, I said, looking to the brazier. The smoke had stopped rising from the ash and the cloud was roiling toward us. My heart dropped into my stomach.

Stay calm, Sion said. *If you panic, you'll only make things worse.*

She had a point, but it was hard not to panic knowing what the enenra was capable of. I sprinted across the cavern, weaving between the stalagmites until I reached the darkness. Sion followed me, but she had to take the pathway as she couldn't fit between the stone pillars.

I can't see anything, I complained, feeling my way forward cautiously. The surface of the stalagmites was surprisingly smooth despite their rough appearance.

Keep moving. The enenra is getting closer.

My foot caught on something and I fell forward, landing roughly on the ground. A moment later, the top of one of the stalagmites was ripped away by the cloud of smoke. There was a whistling sound as it flew through the air, which ended in an abrupt crash as it struck something and shattered.

I stayed on my hands and knees and crawled forward until I reached the wall, then rose to my feet and searched for an exit. It started to sink in that I was probably wrong. There was no other doorway, not even a tunnel or an adjoining cave.

Sion roared and flames illuminated the darkness. The enenra was hovering near the ceiling, a hideous face with glowing blue eyes staring down at her. Sion ducked her head as the enenra swiped at her, narrowly missing her neck. The creature's form dissolved into smoke and drifted lower. Sion growled and whipped her tail at the cloud, but her appendage passed through it.

I turned away, knowing there was nothing I could do to assist Sion. I focused on finding another exit, but as I blindly felt along the wall and reached the end, it became apparent that the bronze doors were the only way out. Cursing under my breath, I made my way back through the maze of stalagmites to the doors.

No luck on another exit, I told Sion. *I think we're trapped.*

I'll keep this thing busy, but keep trying to open the doors. If we can't get them open, I fear we shall both die in here.

I didn't know what she expected me to do. If she couldn't break the doors, then I certainly couldn't. If only I were a sorcerer like Maren.

Maren.

My heart stung with the pain of knowing she was trapped on that cursed boat, while I was trapped here with no hope of escape. If I died here, Maren would never be free. I couldn't let that happen. I *refused* to let that happen. I looked at the brazier, an idea coming to me. It was probably foolish and wouldn't even work, but my options had run out.

I raced to the brazier, holding back my revulsion as I dug around in the ashes. Sion roared behind me, and I knew time was running out. I touched something hard and grabbed onto it, pulling it free. It was a bone, exactly what I was looking for. I dropped it to the ground and unsheathed my sword, then pressed the tip of the blade against it.

"Please let this do something," I prayed softly, then forced the sword down with all my strength.

The blade cut into the bone, shearing a straight line down the middle. An unearthly screech filled the chamber. I looked to where Sion was and saw the enenra's smoky form had solidified. Sion quickly lashed her tail at it, and the creature was thrown against the cavern wall.

It worked!

Keep up whatever you're doing, Sion said. *I think that blow actually hurt it.*

I pulled my sword free and the enenra turned

back into smoke, darting away from Sion and coming toward me. I stabbed the blade down into the bone. The enenra cried out again, but it wasn't as loud this time. The amount of time its form solidified was also shorter. Sion managed to rake her claws into its back before it turned into a cloud and continued rushing at me.

My final strike cut the bone in half, but it didn't affect the enenra at all. Panicked, I fished another bone from the brazier and struck it. The enenra became solid again, its blue eyes burning with hatred. Sion attacked, clawing and snapping at the creature's flesh. There was no blood, but the enenra howled in agony and turned around, delivering a powerful blow to the side of Sion's head.

I watched in horror as Sion collapsed, her massive form going still. Her presence was still in the bond, and I heaved a sigh of relief that she was alive, but now it was just me and the enenra. I drove my sword into the bone, buying me enough time to grab another bone from the brazier. When I looked up, the enenra was gone.

Had I banished it somehow? Or was it merely hiding in the darkness?

Carrying the bone in one hand and my sword in the other, I rushed across the cavern to Sion. She was breathing, but unconscious. I eyed the ceiling, watching for the enenra, but it was nowhere to be seen.

Something crashed against the doors and I snapped my gaze at them. Whatever it was, it was trying to get in, not out. I gripped the hilt of my blade tightly, wondering what sort of other creatures were down here. Were there two enenra?

There was a second crash, followed by a third. The doors burst open, revealing Katori and Domori. Katori spotted me and I shook my head, trying to warn her from coming into the cavern.

"Run!" I screamed.

A smoky cloud appeared in the air above me, and the enenra wailed gleefully. I struck my sword against the bone, then quickly pulled the collar from my belt and latched it around Sion's neck. Within moments, she was in human form, naked and vulnerable. I sheathed my sword and picked her up, then ran as quickly as I could toward the doors.

"Hurry!" Katori shouted, staring at the enenra behind me.

My mind told my legs to work harder, but my muscles refused to obey. It was all I could do just to jog. I reached the doors and crossed the threshold, falling to my knees. I set Sion on the floor and got back to my feet, helping Katori and Domori push the massive doors closed.

"That brace goes on the doors," I said, hurrying to the wooden block that Sion had removed earlier.

Domori helped me lift the thing, which seemed far heavier than was possible, and we successfully set it into the brackets attached to the doors. On the other side, the enenra pushed against them, but they held firm.

"What happened?" Katori asked, looking at Sion's unmoving body.

"The enenra struck her," I said. "It's real. The blasted thing is real!"

"I told you it was. This is why we should never have come down here."

"Did you get that other door open?" I asked.

"Yes. I was going to wait for you, but I went into the room to see what was hidden there. Eldwin, there was so much magic in there I nearly fainted."

"That's a good thing," I said. "We can take it all with us."

"It's too much to carry," Katori replied. "It will take a couple of trips, and once we leave, I don't want to come back down here."

"Sion can help carry some of it."

"I think that we will be carrying Sion, judging by the look of her."

"She'll be fine," I said, though I sounded more confident than I felt.

"Domori and I put most of the items into sacks and set them near the pedestal that held the scepter. I think we should take as much as we can carry and leave this place."

I looked at Sion and she stirred, her eyes blinking a few times. If I had to come back down here myself to get the items we needed, then so be it.

"Fine. Let's get the bags and get back aboveground."

Are you all right? I asked Sion.

A little fuzzy, but I've taken more abuse before.

Are you fit to carry anything?

I can manage.

"We have a problem," Domori said.

Katori and I looked at him, but he didn't need to say anything. Tendrils of smoke were slipping under the door.

5

"We need to be swift," Katori said, then she took the lead as we rushed away from the doors.

I grabbed the bag I'd left before entering the cavern and we ran along the hall, our stomping feet echoing off the walls. I felt bad for Sion. She was still naked, and while dragons didn't think about nudity as humans did, it still felt odd to see her sprinting nude.

Katori turned left, and we continued onward into the prayer garden. I continuously looked over my shoulder, expecting to see the enenra right behind us. Luck, or something else, was on our side, however, and there was no sign of the creature. My relief quickly turned to dread when I considered that the enenra may have chosen to flee the temple altogether. If that thing was free to terrorize the countryside, it would be all but impossible to stop it.

"What if the enenra gets out of the temple?" I asked.

"I'd rather not consider that possibility," Katori huffed. "Let us overcome one problem at a time."

While I understood her sentiment and agreed with it, that didn't change the fact that we were unprepared for something like that. We needed a plan of action just in case.

"We're almost there," Katori said. "Once we get

the sacks, we must flee as quickly as we can. Once the wards are restored on the main door, the enenra won't be able to escape."

As soon as we stepped into the room where Katori had left the items, I almost fell over. Despite not having any magical inclination, I felt a wall of power so thick that it was like running into a real barrier. I shook my head, trying to clear it, and surveyed the number of sacks they'd collected. There were at least a dozen, and each one was full.

"If this isn't enough magic to make a bridge, then I don't know what we'll do," I said.

"Let us hope it is," Katori replied.

She looked at each of us, then at the sacks.

"I don't think we can carry them all out. Sion can't transform back into her dragon form without getting stuck or destroying the temple. We'll have to leave some of it behind."

"I can carry more than you three combined," Sion said. "Tie some of them together and I'll do the rest."

Domori went to work cutting an empty sack into strips. He used them as a makeshift rope, looping a strip around the top of a bag, then tying it to another strip. He repeated the process until most of the sacks were held together in two piles, then he used a thicker, longer strap to connect them.

I stood at the doorway, keeping watch for the enenra. Wherever the creature was, it hadn't shown its face yet.

"Where's your robe?" Katori asked.

"We left it in the cavern," Sion answered. "I am not troubled by my appearance."

"No, but I am. Here."

Katori grabbed an empty sack and cut some holes into the material so that Sion could wear it like a long shirt, then handed it to her. Sion slipped it on over her head and adjusted it.

"You look like a homeless person," I said, smiling.

"Or a person in mourning," Katori replied.

Odd sounds echoed into the chamber, sending a chill up my spine.

"This is taking too long," I said. "We need to get moving."

Sion knelt near the sacks and Domori placed the rope along Sion's shoulders. She grabbed onto the strips where they connected to the sacks and stood, easily lifting them off the floor.

"I am ready," she said.

"That makes one of us."

I rushed over to grab one of the remaining sacks and dumped the items from mine into it, then struggled to keep from dropping the full one as we hurried out of the room and back into the prayer garden. More sounds reached my ears, and I feared that we were walking into a trap laid by the enenra. In our favor, though, the glowing walls illuminated most everything, leaving few shadows for the creature to hide among.

Katori must have gotten turned around, for we entered a hall that ended in rubble. Stone and dirt closed off the area, and we were forced to backtrack. Sion sniffed the air and nodded.

"That way."

We continued in the direction she indicated and found ourselves in the correct place. It was the chamber leading to the entrance, but something felt off. I slowed my pace, glancing around the room.

"What is it?" Katori asked.

"I'm not sure. Sion, do you sense the enenra?"

"Yes, but not here. It's nearby."

Perhaps I was worried about nothing, but in my experience, ignoring your gut feelings usually ended up being a mistake. I didn't see anything to cause concern, but I *felt* something. It was dark, too. Evil, even.

The sound of footsteps signaled the approach of someone. From the door leading to the antechamber of the exit, a robed figure came into view, followed by several men. I recognized one of them as Akada, one of the two men who had attacked me before I found Katori. That led me to assume the robed figure was Kage. Silence descended on the room as our groups eyed one another.

"What are you doing here?" Katori finally spoke.

"Isn't it obvious? I'm here for the dragon."

Kage's voice was soft and smooth like silk. The hood of his robes was pulled over his head and I was unable to see his face.

"You can't have her," I said.

"You must be the rider from the north. Akada told me about you and your … deformity."

My cheeks flushed with heat. Despite having proven myself time and time again, it still upset me when people mentioned my mangled arm.

"You will hand over your dragon now or you will all perish."

We were outnumbered, though I considered Sion easily worth more than Kage and his ten men. The only problem was that we weren't outside of the temple yet. I glanced up at the ceiling and knew by the height it wouldn't be a good idea to remove her collar yet.

"You are reduced to idle threats?" Katori set her bag down and stepped forward. "When did the powerful Kage become little more than a tyrant?"

"Ah, Katori. You mistake my strength for tyranny. I do not want to terrorize, but to unite. I want to bring the dragon riders under one banner and solidify our place as rulers. Not every man can bond with a dragon. Why should the few, the powerful, be forced to serve the lesser among us? No, that is a perversion of nature. Under my guidance, we will become stronger. We will take back what is ours and restore the natural order."

Kage was clearly insane. That, or he was

delusional. Regardless, he wasn't taking Sion from me. Domori drew his sword and gave it to Katori. She swung the blade in a practiced fashion.

"We will settle this once and for all."

"You will do what your master would not?" Kage drew his sword, a curved single-edged blade.

"I will do what my master *could* not do," Katori clarified.

I looked at Sion and lowered my voice. "Where is the enenra?"

"It's close, but I think it's waiting for something."

What would an unstoppable creature be waiting on? It could slaughter us all with barely any effort. I didn't like this, but I knew we couldn't get past Kage and his men without a fight. I set my bag down beside Sion and drew my sword.

Katori and Kage stood silently for a moment, watching each other. Without any warning, Katori rushed ahead, swinging her blade. Kage whirled in a circle, bringing his sword up to block Katori's strike. His robes billowed as he moved, and at first, I thought it would hinder his movements. As I watched him and Katori battle, I realized I was wrong. The billowing material caused Katori to think she struck him when she hadn't, which allowed Kage to take the advantage.

He whirled his blade in a frenzy, moving it so quickly that I barely saw anything other than the flicker of light off of the blade. Domori rushed past me, drawing a long dagger from his belt. He engaged the nearest man, which happened to be Akada. The ringing of steel pierced the air, and two of Kage's men rushed to help their fellow against Domori.

I couldn't just stand there and watch, so I joined the fray, slashing and jabbing with my blade. Kage's men were hardly wearing any armor, but it swiftly became evident why. They were faster and more skilled with their blades than I was, using techniques I'd never seen before. I managed to hit one man on the arm, slicing a gash along his elbow, but it was hardly life-threatening.

He retreated to the back of the group and another man took his place, putting me on the defensive. His blows made my arms tremor as I blocked and backstepped. It was taking everything I had just to keep from dropping my sword.

"Eldwin!"

Sion's cry sent a jolt of fear through me. I slipped past my attacker's guard as his sword swung wide, slamming my booted foot into his kneecap. I felt and heard the crack as his leg bent awkwardly. He cried out as he toppled over, and I looked at Sion to see what was wrong.

Funneling into the chamber was the smoky cloud of the enenra.

6

The creature hovered near the ceiling, its glowing eyes burning with fury.

A few of Kage's men noticed the enenra's presence and began pointing and shouting. I retreated to Sion's side and sheathed my blade, knowing it would do nothing to harm the creature. Kage's men didn't know that, and they rushed toward it, brandishing their weapons.

I picked up my bag and waited for a path to the exit to be clear. Katori and Kage continued to battle, likely unaware of the enenra. As the chamber filled with the screams of the dying, Katori pulled back from the battle. The creature's timing couldn't have been better, as it looked like Katori's strength was flagging.

Kage rallied the rest of his men and they attacked the enenra, but the creature's smoky form eluded their strikes. It appeared here and there, slashing its way through Kage's ranks. With the exit clear, Katori led us into the antechamber. Haruna was lying on the ground in a puddle of blood, dead. It was obvious by his wounds that Kage's men had killed him.

Katori knelt beside him and whispered a prayer, her fingers closing his lifeless eyes. The rest of us stood outside the bronze doors. I didn't want to rush her, but we needed to seal the wards before the enenra escaped. I opened my mouth to say something when Katori stood and hurried out into the tunnel, clutching the amulet she'd given Haruna. Domori and I pushed one of the doors closed, but before we could get to the other one, Kage came sprinting toward us.

He was alone and covered in blood. I struggled to draw my blade from its sheath, but Kage dodged around us and continued past, disappearing down the dark passageway.

"Hurry!" Katori urged.

We closed the second door and Katori placed the amulet into the space along the crevice of the doors. She held it there for a long while, and I listened intently, expecting to hear the enenra crashing against the doors at any moment.

There was only silence.

"It is done," Katori said. "The wards have been restored."

I breathed a sigh of relief and sat down on the ground.

"I thought we were going to die in there," I admitted.

"We almost did," Sion said. "The enenra is a powerful enemy."

"I know how it was created."

Katori looked at me curiously. I related the vision Sion and I had seen, and Katori frowned.

"It is true, then. The followers of *Ho-musubi*

were wicked."

"From what I saw, that's an understatement. No wonder the enenra is so enraged. It was once an innocent man, sacrificed for no reason."

It grew quiet, but the knowledge that Maren was waiting on me spurred me to ignore my exhaustion. I got back on my feet and removed the collar from Sion. She shifted back into her dragon form, and for the first time in months, her scales were a vibrant red color.

It's the magic, Sion said, reading my thoughts. *It's rejuvenating my spirit.*

Hopefully, this bridge idea works and we can fix everything.

Hope is better than fear, Sion replied.

I turned to Katori.

"Thank you for everything. I wish we could stay longer, but we need to get to Maren and figure out how to unravel the spells on these items."

"We will go with you," Katori said.

"What about Kage?"

"I will deal with him once we are done."

"I would love to have you," I said, "but I think Sion will be hard-pressed to carry me and these bags."

"We can ride Demris."

I'd almost forgotten that he was here at the school.

"If he will allow it, then I would be honored to have your help. I think we're all in over our heads in this situation."

Katori nodded solemnly. "These are trying times. The restoration of magic will be a major aid in returning to normal … if that is something we can achieve."

I didn't know whether she was referring to achieving normalcy or creating the bridge to the island, and I suspected that I wouldn't like her answer. I kept my mouth shut and nodded. Using the makeshift ropes Domori had created for the bags, we placed the ropes across Sion's back, using the saddle to help secure them against her sides.

Once they were in place, we traveled along the tunnel in silence until we reached the cave that Demris was in. He lifted his head as we approached, and I was glad to see that Kage's men hadn't messed with him.

Can you ask him if he will carry them to the coast? I asked Sion.

Yes.

I wasn't sure if Demris was still upset with me, but he showed no signs if he was. After a few moments, Demris rose to his feet.

Demris has agreed to carry them, but only because they are going to help Maren.

Thank him for me.

Tell him yourself.

"Thank you for your help, Demris."

The enormous green dragon stared at me, but there was no anger in his eyes. He stepped out of the cave and followed us through the tunnel. We reached the exit and I breathed deeply of the fresh air. The temperature was warmer aboveground, too. We made our way around to the front of the school.

"I will gather some food. Do you need water?"

Katori pointed to Sion's saddle where my water skin was attached. It was almost empty, so I pulled it free and handed it to her. She and Domori went inside the school, leaving me with Sion and Demris.

What if this doesn't work? I asked Sion.

Then we will find another way.

What if there isn't one?

Why are humans so obsessed with focusing on the negative? It must make for a dreary existence.

I chuckled. She was right, of course.

It's just our nature, I think. I'll try to change my thinking.

Change is good, Sion said.

Katori returned with my waterskin, as well as three small packs of food. I glanced inside and saw it was mostly fish and several golden-brown balls.

"What are those?" I asked, holding one up.

"Rice balls."

I gave her a confused look.

"It is rice wrapped in seaweed."

"I can understand why you just call them rice balls. The idea of eating seaweed is … different."

Katori smiled. She was a beautiful woman, though the trials she had suffered since I'd last seen her had buried that beauty beneath a layer of grief. I wasn't sure why, but I felt the urge to hug her, so I did. She hesitantly returned the gesture, and I wondered if I had crossed some sort of cultural line.

"Thank you," she whispered.

I released her and nodded, feeling awkward.

"I think we're ready."

Domori returned, his helmet tucked under his arm. He avoided my gaze, and I spotted what appeared to be a tear on his cheek. I swallowed hard, realizing that he must be grieving for Haruna. Seeing someone as strong as Domori in a sad state tore at my heart in a way I didn't expect. I cleared my throat.

"Sion and I will lead the way," I announced.

Demris said he'll race us. I think we can beat him this time.

I don't think that's a good idea. What if we drop a bag? The items will be scattered everywhere.

Sion rumbled in disagreement but she didn't argue. I was about to climb into the saddle when Sion perked her head to the side, sniffing the air.

Someone's coming.

I followed her gaze to the main gate.

Is it Kage?

No.

A small child entered the courtyard. She was dirty and disheveled, her clothes covered in dust. Her feet were bare of any shoes and she walked with a limp. I guessed that she couldn't be older than twelve.

"There's a child here," I said lowly, looking at Katori.

She turned around and the child froze.

"Master K-Katori?" the girl stuttered.

"Yes, child. What are you doing here?"

"We need your help."

"Come closer."

The girl nodded and slowly closed the distance. I could see her feet were bloody and my heart fell into my stomach. Where were her shoes? How far had she walked to get here?

"Who needs my help?" Katori asked, kneeling so she was level with the girl.

"Our town. I walked for two days to come here. My mother told me to find you."

"Where is your mother? Why didn't she come with you?"

The girl heaved in a breath and I thought she was going to burst into tears. "My mother is gone."

"I am sorry," Katori replied. "Why did she send you here?"

"The dead are rising from their graves."

7

Did I hear that right?

She said the dead are rising, Sion replied.

That's what I thought.

Katori brushed a tear from the girl's cheek with one of her fingers.

"What do you mean?"

"The people who have passed on to the spirit world are coming out of their graves. They attacked our town and killed many people."

I tried to envision what the girl described, but it was a stretch. To my knowledge, the only person to come back from the dead was the False King, and that was only by the power of the Necromancer. Had someone else discovered his dark magic?

Dark magic is a scourge upon the land, Sion said.

I know. My eyes widened. *What if it isn't dark magic?*

What else could it be?

It could be the souls that are stuck here.

Sion's concern flooded the bond, echoing my own feelings.

"Did you notice anything strange before it happened?" Katori questioned. "Did your mother say anything?"

"A few weeks ago, there were men that had been doing strange things near the burial grounds. The elders thought they were thieves and ran them off, but the men didn't take anything. They were scary looking. My mother only told me to find you. There are rumors that the dragon riders are gone, but I came here first. The dead were everywhere when I escaped. I didn't want to leave my mother, but she made me. I saw one of them attack her." The girl trembled. "She was trying to fight it off. I couldn't watch."

Katori embraced the girl, looking back at me. The apprehension I felt was reflected on her face. She released the girl and stood, coming over to me.

"We need to see if what she says is true," Katori whispered.

"I don't disagree, but we need to go to the coast first. If the dead really are rising, then having magic back will help."

"We can't wait that long. We don't even know if this will work. I won't let innocent people die."

"It *must* work," I replied. "We have no other options at this point."

"We are going to her town first."

"What if we take the items to Maren and then check it out?"

"No." Katori crossed her arms, her expression one of dead-set defiance.

She reminded me of Maren. She could be stubborn when she wanted, and once she'd made a decision about something, it was pointless arguing with her.

"How about a compromise? Domori and Demris can take this stuff to the coast, and you and I will go and see these dead people."

"That is fair," Katori said. "But the girl needs to be taken somewhere safe first."

I resisted the urge to argue and nodded instead.

Is Demris fine with this arrangement? I asked Sion.

Yes. He wants to see Maren.

"Let them go now, and we can take the girl somewhere. With any luck, this will all be a wild tale from the mouth of a child."

"Since when has luck been on our side? No, I fear that we have found another problem that needs our hands."

I didn't acknowledge her fears, mainly because I had a feeling that she was right. Domori and I worked to remove the bags from Sion and put them on Demris. He watched us work, seeming to be patient, but his tail continuously flicked back and forth like a cat ready to spring into action.

Once all the bags had been moved, Domori climbed into the saddle and Demris launched into the air, his powerful wings stirring up the dirt in the courtyard. I was forced to close my eyes and bury my mouth in the crook of my arm to keep from getting a mouthful of dust.

"Do you have family that lives near your town?" Katori asked the girl.

"Yes. My grandparents live in the farming village to the east of us."

"We will take you there to stay with them. They will not turn you away, will they?"

"No, Master Katori. I am close to them and we visit regularly."

"Good. Where is your home?"

"Taurugi."

Katori nodded. "I know where it is." She looked at me. "I think Kage is behind this somehow."

"Really? I assumed it had to do with the buildup of souls."

We stared at each other in silence for a moment, each realizing there could be more reasons for the dead to rise than we suspected.

"Regardless of who or what is causing it, we must stop it."

If the souls were the cause, then there would be nothing we could do to stop it without magic. I bit my tongue and decided to let Katori take the lead. If she was wrong, the blame wouldn't be on my shoulders.

Can you carry all three of us? I asked Sion.

Yes. The girl is small and looks light.

What about the disruption to magic? I don't want you to fall out of the sky.

I feel fine after being around all that magic, but we should move quickly. Just in case.

"Ladies first," I said, motioning to Katori.

She gracefully climbed up Sion's shoulder, then held onto the saddle as she reached her hand down.

"Lift the girl to me."

I did so, lifting her by the waist. She was lighter than I expected which made the task easy. Katori placed the girl in front of her, then I climbed up and sat in the front.

"Which way is Taurugi?"

"East," Katori replied, pointing past the gates. "It's an hour by dragon flight. We'll take the girl to the farming village first and circle back."

We're ready when you are, I told Sion.

Hold on!

Leaving the ground was always exhilarating to me. Sion hunched down, clawing into the stones of the courtyard. She stretched her wings and leaped into the air, her muscles flexing as she flapped to gain altitude. Within moments, we were high above the ground, speeding to the east.

As we flew, my thoughts turned to Maren. She was strong and courageous, which was just one of the reasons I loved her. I also secretly loved her stubbornness, though I would never tell her that. My lips slowly crept upward until I was smiling. Maren was somehow … perfect. The fact that she returned my feelings was hard to fathom some days.

When you are done romanticizing, could you take a look at what I'm seeing?

Sion's voice inside my head shattered my daydreaming and I peered down at the landscape below. Taurugi was small, but just as majestic as everything else in Terran. The elegant, flowing architecture of the buildings was the same as that of the school, and the buildings accented the scenery around them rather than taking away from it. Everything appeared normal from my vantage point.

It's abandoned, Sion noted.

Is it? I squinted as if that would help me see better, but the details were too small for me to make out.

"The town is empty!" I shouted over my shoulder.

"Continue to the farming village! It's not much farther!"

Sion flapped her wings, increasing her speed. We left Taurugi behind and quickly spotted the rice fields that surrounded the small village. There didn't appear to be anyone working the fields, and I didn't see movement in the village, either.

Is it also abandoned?

No, Sion replied. *I can smell people down there. And something else.*

What?

Death and decay.

Her words sent a chill along my spine, but I quickly shook it off.

Take us down.

Sion tilted to the right and began a slow, spiraling descent. She landed a fair distance away from the village, but also avoided the rice fields. She chose a small plot of hard-packed dirt that appeared to be where children played. Small toys littered the area, along with footprints.

If this place isn't abandoned, where is everyone?

They're here, Sion confirmed. *Probably hiding.*

"Stay here," I told Katori. "I'll take a look around and make sure it's safe to bring the girl down."

I jumped from the saddle onto the ground and drew my blade.

Tell me if you see anything.

Of course.

I walked toward the village, my senses on high alert. Natural sounds reached my ears, but I didn't hear people talking or children playing. Perhaps Sion was right and they were hiding in fear. As I got closer to the village, I realized that was exactly the case. The buildings all had their windows covered with bamboo from the outside.

Something foul-smelling was in the air and I scrunched my nose. I approached one of the homes and knocked on the door, but there was no reply.

"Is anyone here?" I called out. "I'm a dragon rider."

Silence.

I shrugged and went to the next house, with the same results. I continued through the village, examining the homes. They were all locked down securely. Sion said she could smell people here, but I was starting to think she'd been mistaken. As I reached the edge of the village where the rice fields began, I spotted someone standing in the field. Their back was to me, so I walked closer, purposely splashing loudly through the watery field so they heard me approaching.

"Sir! Where is everyone?"

The foul smell intensified the closer I got. When the man turned around, my eyes widened in terror and disgust. The flesh of his face was mostly gone, the whiteness of his bones showing. I stopped mid-step and almost dropped my sword.

The man snarled and raced toward me.

8

I backpedaled, adjusting my grip on the hilt of my blade and bringing it up to defend myself. It was hard to believe what I was seeing. A corpse risen from the dead. Its glowing eyes had an intelligence in them as if it knew I was afraid.

It reached for me, but I swung my sword in a half-circle and cut its hand off. If the corpse felt pain, it didn't show it as it continued trying to strike me with its stump. My foot hit something under the water and I fell backward, landing with a splash.

The corpse was on top of me immediately, its mouth snapping at my face. A piece of rotting flesh fell off its face and landed on my cheek, making me gag as I struggled to push the corpse off of me.

I grabbed the end of my blade with my left hand and pushed the sword up, using it to keep the undead man away from my face. My arm muscles burned with the exertion and I knew I couldn't keep it at bay for long.

A whistling sound filled the air and an arrow struck the corpse in the chest. A second later, there was another whistle and a second arrow struck the corpse in the center of its forehead. The dead man ceased moving and his weight sagged against me. I rolled his body off of me and stood up, looking in the direction where the arrows had come from.

The door to one of the homes was open and a

young woman stood in front of it. She was holding a bow and had another arrow ready.

"Hurry! Before the others come!"

"Others?"

My question was answered as a hand grabbed onto my ankle. The thing I had tripped over was another risen corpse. Its head broke the surface of the water and it bit me. My boot protected my leg, and I smacked the undead thing in the head with my sword, jerking my leg free of its grasp.

"The head!" the woman shouted.

I swiftly jabbed my blade into the corpse's skull. It went still and I pulled my blade free.

"Hurry!"

I glanced behind me and saw more corpses rising from the watery field. I sheathed my blade and ran for the open door. As soon as I was inside, the woman slammed the door shut and latched it.

The girl was right, I told Sion. *The dead have risen somehow. Take to the air!*

I'm already flying, Sion replied. *We saw them coming out of the water. I will flame them all.*

Not yet. I found a survivor. Let me talk with her first.

Sion grumbled but didn't argue. I turned my attention to the woman who'd helped me. She was shorter than me, though not by much. Her black hair stretched down past her shoulders, but it was tied in place with a ribbon. She was staring at me expectantly.

"What is it?" I asked.

"I said what is your name."

"Sorry, I was communicating with my dragon. I'm Eldwin."

"My name is Reika. You're a dragon rider?"

"Yes. I'm from Osnen."

"What are you doing here?"

I paused, not sure how to interpret her tone. "We've come to see what was happening in Taurugi. A girl came to the school with a tale of the risen dead. Now I see what she meant."

"Niroko made it?" Reika looked relieved. "Her mother will be happy to hear it."

"She's all right," I replied. "She's here with Katori."

"Master Katori is here? Where?"

"They are both on my dragon, Sion. She's flying over the village. Do you know Master Katori?"

"Yes. I was a dragon rider before the sickness claimed my dragon."

"I'm sorry for your loss."

Reika bowed her head. "Thank you."

Something heavy started hitting the door, which caused me to flinch. I shook my head.

"What happened here? Niroko said that the dead

attacked Taurugi."

"It's a confusing story, but from what I have gathered, the dead are from the graves of Taurugi. People were doing something to the graves and shortly after, the bodies clawed their way free."

"That's what Niroko told us. I was hoping for more information."

"That's all I have. Most of the people here are farmers, but a handful of survivors from Taurugi managed to make it here before the dead did. They didn't have much information to share. We've been trapped indoors ever since."

"When was that?"

"Two days ago."

I frowned. As it stood, it sounded like Katori might be right about Kage being behind it all. Still, we needed to find out for sure, but I didn't know how we would determine that.

"Are there any other warriors here?"

"No. I came here to see my family before I planned to go to the Elder Dragons."

"How important are the rice fields to these people?" I asked.

"They are a matter of life or death. Why?"

"My dragon can make quick work of the dead, but I don't want to jeopardize the homes or the crops. How many corpses came here?"

"It's hard to say. Perhaps fifty."

How many do you see? I asked Sion.

There was a moment of silence before she answered. *Fifteen. There may be others under the water.*

"How do you feel about helping clear the village of these things?"

Reika's expression hardened. "It would be an honor."

"Good. Instead of using dragon fire, I think it would be safer to handle them ourselves. I'll have Sion drop Katori down here so she can help us. How many arrows do you have?"

"Not enough, but I'll make due."

Can you get close enough to drop Katori near this house without damaging the buildings?

I can try.

I need a guarantee.

The wind off my wings will probably rip the roofs off.

We'll meet you over where we landed, then. I'll give you the signal when we're about to open the door.

"I'll take the lead," I said. "If they are within a few feet, I'll handle them. Otherwise, take out as many as you can with your bow. Are you ready?"

Reika nodded. I drew my sword and readied myself for what awaited us.

"Open the door."

Reika unlatched it and shoved it open.

Now!

I stepped out and spotted three corpses. One was on the ground, having been knocked down when Reika opened the door. The other two made noises in their throats and rushed me. Now that I was prepared, they didn't seem as frightening. I thrust my sword forward, penetrating the skull of one, then quickly pulled the blade back and swung upward at an angle, cleaving the second corpse's head in two. The third was the easiest to dispatch as it was struggling to get up.

Ahead of us was another one. It was trying to open the door of a house. Reika stepped in front of me, drew her bowstring back, and let an arrow fly. Her aim was immaculate. The arrow struck the corpse in the temple and it collapsed to the ground.

"You're really good with that bow," I said.

"Thank you. I've been practicing for years."

Sion was circling above where she'd landed earlier.

You walk too slow, she complained jokingly.

Well, if I had wings, I'd be fast too.

Reika and I hurried through the village to where Sion was. She landed long enough for me to wave Katori down, then she took to the air again.

"Look who I found." I motioned to Reika, who bowed.

"Master Katori."

"Rise," Katori bade. "Are you all right?"

"Yes, though I cannot say the same for the people here."

"We're going to get rid of these corpses so these people can return to their lives," I said. "We could use your help."

"Do we know how this happened?"

"Not yet. Reika said the people who escaped from Taurugi didn't have much information on how things transpired, so I figured once we clear this place out, we can go see if we can find anything."

"That's a good idea," Katori said.

"Those are the only kind I have."

Reika and Katori stared at me. "If you say so."

Clearly my joke was lost on them.

They're coming from the fields, Sion warned.

I turned around and spotted a large group of dead people coming straight for us.

"It's too bad we don't have any magic," I said, glancing at Katori.

"Yes, it is. That wouldn't be because of any of your great ideas, though, would it?"

My smile faded and I turned my gaze ahead. Well played.

The group of dead were drawing closer. Reika picked a few of them off with deadly accuracy, but there were too many.

"Conserve your arrows. Katori and I will need you to keep watch for us while we take them head-on."

"Shall we make a wager, you and I? Whoever takes down the most wins."

"What do we win?" I asked.

Katori smirked. "Bragging rights."

I laughed. "I'm in."

"Let us cleanse this disease from the village, then."

The horde of dead reached us and everything became a bloodbath.

9

Katori became a blur of motion.

She ducked and rolled, evading the dead easily. Her fluid, graceful movements made me feel clumsy in comparison. I hacked and slashed, removing limbs and dropping corpses as fast as I could. Reika fired off a few arrows over our heads, taking out the stragglers.

I was trying to keep count of how many I slew, but I gave up when I saw the pile growing at Katori's feet. She was wielding the sword that Domori had given her in the temple, and a metallic ring sounded every time she struck a corpse.

Sion's shadow blanketed us as she flew overhead, and I could feel her envy in the bond. She wanted to scorch the undead with her fire, but she stayed in the air and watched over us. A corpse managed to get close enough to land a hit, striking me in the shoulder. It didn't hurt, but it threw my balance off and I staggered to the side, right into the arms of another corpse.

Reika pulled an arrow from her quiver and leaped forward, jabbing the steel tip into its eye socket. The corpse collapsed and I offered her a quick nod of thanks before thrusting my sword into the neck of another undead. Its head came free and rolled on the ground.

"You're losing!" Katori shouted as she

sidestepped a swing.

"We're not through yet!"

I leaped over the pile of bodies to engage a smaller group that had joined the fray. A few thrusts later and they were all down, joining their fellows in the dirt. It felt like an eternity before we'd cut them all down, yet at the same time, it seemed like we'd only just begun. Katori and I were both surrounded by bodies, but it was clear she was the winner of our bet.

"Last one," Reika said, aiming her bow at me.

Before I could move out of the way, she released her arrow. It whizzed past my head, a brush of air tickling my ear. I looked over my shoulder just in time to see her arrow thud into the face of a corpse that seemed more alive than the others. It dropped to its knees before landing face-first in the dust.

"You didn't give me time to move," I said.

"You didn't need to move," Reika replied. "I wouldn't have taken the shot if I thought I would hit you."

"I felt the air from the arrow. That was too close for comfort."

"You're alive, aren't you? What is there to complain about?"

I shrugged. "I guess you're right. Did we get them all?"

"If not, there aren't many left. It was a sight to

behold to see you in action, Master Katori."

Katori wiped her blade on one of the corpses and looked around the village.

"I do not bask in praise, so I will take your words as a compliment from one skilled warrior to another," she said, offering a slight bow to Reika. "There is no one else who has a mastery of the bow as you do."

"Thank you, Master."

"I'm glad we're on the same side," I said. "I'd hate to be on the other end of your wrath. Either of you."

Katori smiled. "As you should."

"I will let the people know it is safe now. You are welcome to stay at my parents' home. There is food, and you can use their water to clean yourselves."

"We probably should continue to Taurugi," I said. "We have another pressing matter to attend to after this one."

"May I have a moment alone with Reika?" Katori asked.

"Of course. I'll go clean up."

You can bring Niroko down now. Her mother is here somewhere.

Her mother lives? That is good.

I returned to Reika's home and used the basin to wash my face and my hands, then I cleaned my blade off and sheathed it. Katori entered as I was leaving and I joined Sion at the edge of the village. Reika took Niroko to one of the homes and an older woman wrapped the girl tightly in a hug. I was glad to see her mother had survived. That was one small victory, at least.

Katori returned a short while later, looking more like how I remembered her. Her eyes even seemed to have a spark in them, replacing the haunted look that had been there.

"Until we see evidence otherwise, I'm convinced Kage is responsible for this."

"Perhaps we'll find our answer in Taurugi," I said. "Are you ready to go?"

"Yes, but there's something I'd like to see first."

"What's that?"

"These corpses on fire."

I looked at Sion. "I don't think that will be a problem."

We climbed into the saddle and Sion turned her back toward the village. Inhaling a deep breath, she exhaled a wave of flames onto the corpses, roasting them until there was nothing left but ash.

Satisfied? Sion asked.

Yes. Can you take us to Taurugi?

Only if I get to flame corpses. Walking ones.

If there are any, you have first claim.

Sion hummed, pleased. She launched into the

air, heading west. Within a few minutes, Taurugi was in sight. In the center of the town was a large open square, and Sion took us down there, landing lightly. Unlike the farming village, the buildings here were built with stronger materials and the wind from Sion's wings didn't cause any damage.

I dismounted and eyed the empty streets, keeping my hand on the hilt of my sword. Once Katori joined me on the ground, she motioned toward one of the streets that led between two buildings.

"The burial ground is this way."

We walked along the street in silence, both of us keeping careful watch on our surroundings. There were no sounds aside from birds and other natural things, but I'd learned a nearly fatal lesson in the rice fields. The undead could be anywhere.

"There," Katori said, pointing.

A rectangular plot of land was surrounded by a wall roughly two-feet in height, and an ornate gate was open, allowing free access. Katori entered first. I stood at the gate, half expecting an army of undead to rise from the graves.

Yet nothing happened.

I tentatively stepped into the cemetery and glanced around. There were lines of headstones, all evenly spaced. There was a mausoleum as well, but it was only large enough for one family. Everything seemed undisturbed except for one long line of graves. The plots were open, fresh dirt piled to the sides.

"If Kage is responsible for this, how did he manage it? There's no magic. And why only this row? What about the others? Why not raise an entire legion?"

Katori stood quietly for a moment, staring at the empty graves.

"I know why he chose this row," she finally said.

"Why?"

"This row is the Sakurano family line. My ancestors."

My heart broke for her. Although I didn't know much about him, Kage's hatred had crossed a boundary I would never have expected. He'd raised her dead family members knowing that she would defend the people of Terran against them. He'd forced her to essentially kill her own family. Technically, they were already dead, but still. That was utterly evil.

"I'm sorry," I whispered.

"Kage will pay for this with his life. My master may not have found death to be a useful tool, but I am different."

"I still don't understand how he did this without magic. There must be some other way he accomplished raising the dead. Is there anything that you know of that he could have used?"

"No, nothing I can think of. Necromancy is

forbidden in Terran, but that doesn't mean he didn't learn it in secret."

"That's true, but without magic readily available, he still couldn't cast any spells."

"I don't have the answer, Eldwin."

Her accent made my name sound exotic and I smiled.

Do you know how someone could raise the dead without proper magic? I asked Sion.

Perhaps he used other items as you plan to do for the bridge.

I hadn't considered that. I chewed on my lower lip, thinking.

If only there was a way to know for certain how he did it.

How would that help us?

It would at least confirm if he used necromancy. And then we would know what to expect from him in the future, and how to combat it.

"Reika said the attack on the village happened two days ago. That was before we went into the temple, so he must have had something to power his magic. Do you think Kage knew there was stuff down in the temple he could use to power his magic? Or do you think he happened to follow us by chance?"

"Either scenario seems possible, but perhaps it was the first. You and Maren knew about the items in the temple."

"Yes, but we got that information from a ghost. Without the ferryman telling us, we would never have known. If he knew something was down there, someone had to have told him."

"Maybe he spoke with the souls as well?"

"I suppose that's possible."

I took a step closer to where Katori stood and felt a surge of power course through me. It was coming from the bond, and it was the same power I felt when I battled the basilisk. My vision darkened momentarily, and then I saw the shadowy forms of a group of men.

One of them was Kage.

10

"What are we doing here?"

It was one of Kage's men. I'd seen him in the temple. He'd been one of the first to fall to the enenra's wrath. I glanced around, trying to figure out what was happening. Kage and his men were more like shadows than physically present, and their appearance seemed distorted somehow.

Katori was looking at me. Her mouth was moving, but I couldn't hear what she was saying.

Sion?

I'm here.

Is this a vision like the one in the temple?

I'm not sure. There's a strange magic flowing through the bond, and the vision is being powered by it. Are you doing this?

No, I replied. *At least, not consciously. If it's me, I have no idea how I'm doing it.*

"I told you, we're going to create a thorn in Katori's side. With the dragons dead and her riders scattered in self-imposed exile, she'll have to pull the thorn out alone. And if she happens to die in the process, so be it."

"Where is this thorn you speak of? We're standing in a cemetery."

"Patience is a virtue, Shikō. Why do you think

I've been biding my time? Do you think I enjoy being forced to wait to seek my revenge? If I were not so patient, I would have already fumbled my opportunity. And I would have already cut your throat for questioning me."

Shikō's face paled at the threat.

"Forgive my insolence," he said. "I too want my revenge and it itches beneath my skin. My impatience forces my tongue to speak folly."

"How eloquent," Kage laughed. The other men laughed as well, though whether it was forced or not, I couldn't tell.

"You are forgiven, Shikō. Do not let it happen again."

Shikō offered a slight bow in return.

"The thorn I speak of is here in this cemetery. Katori's ancestors lie beneath the dirt, and I intend to make them rise from death."

His men looked at each other, whispering among themselves. Again, Shikō spoke up.

"How is this possible? Magic has faded from our grasp."

Kage reached into his robes and withdrew an item I immediately recognized. A dragon bone flute. This flute was somewhat different than the others, though. It was black and covered with silver runes.

"This is how," Kage replied.

"What is that?"

"Don't worry about that. Just know that it is going to channel the magic I need to bring these corpses back to life."

"Where did you get it?" Shikō asked.

"You ask too many questions." Kage eyed Shikō suspiciously for a moment, then turned his attention back to the other men. "Prepare to witness my power."

Kage walked over to the row of headstones that belonged to Katori's family line, stopping at the first grave. He pressed the flute to his lips and breathed into it. The music that came out of the instrument wasn't like the music of the other flutes. It was dark and heavy, the notes conjuring up images of death and destruction in my mind.

The music is a curse, Sion hissed through the bond. *It twists and mangles the flow of magic.*

Yes, it is much different than the other flutes. The tune is so ...

Vile, Sion said. *It's a perversion.*

As Kage continued to play, the music began to make my skin crawl. I shivered and took a step back. Ripples in the air appeared near the end of the flute, and they traveled down to the ground, penetrating the grave. As I watched, the dirt shifted, heaving upward.

A decayed hand broke the surface.

"Gods," I breathed. "They actually did it."

Abomination! Sion screamed into the bond.

The ground bulged until the corpse clawed its way free, rising from the grave. It was a horrific sight. The corpse was all bones, its flesh having decomposed long ago. Kage's men didn't hide their disgust. They backed away from the unholy thing, whispering prayers and making signs of warding in the air.

"It won't harm you," Kage said. "It is bound to me. My will is its purpose."

He pointed to the town. "Go forth and cause chaos."

The corpse did as he commanded. It left the cemetery and disappeared down the street. Kage stepped to the next grave and repeated the process. A few moments later, another corpse freed itself from its grave. Kage went down the entire row, using the dark magic of the flute to raise more and more bodies.

Soon, screams all around the town filled the air. The undead were terrorizing the townspeople. Their cries wrenched at my heart and I silently begged for the vision to end. Once all of the graves were empty, Kage gathered his men and they fled the cemetery. The magic coming from the bond faded. I looked at Katori, but before I could say anything, my entire body weakened and I collapsed into darkness.

When I awoke, I was lying on my back. A large cherry blossom tree towered above me as if standing guard, and a headache pounded within my skull. I sat up and saw Katori was shoveling loose dirt into the empty graves. Judging by where I was lying, she must have moved me. I wanted to help her, but my muscles lacked the strength.

You're awake.

Yes.

Good.

My head is killing me, I said. *I must have hit a rock or something when I passed out.*

I think it's from the magic, Sion replied. *When the flow of it stopped, I felt tired.*

So did I.

Yes, but I think you were channeling it somehow. Perhaps that is why you collapsed. It was feeding off of your strength.

I'm not a sorcerer.

Not that you know of.

I considered the possibility that I might be one for all of a few seconds before discounting the possibility. I hadn't summoned the magic. It had come through the bond of its own accord and used me to fulfill its purpose. I would have to ask Maren about it.

"You're not dead," Katori grunted as she shoveled. "What happened to you? It was like you weren't here."

"I wasn't, in a way. It's difficult to explain, but I saw what happened here. Kage used a dragon bone flute to channel the flow of magic so he could raise the dead."

"I knew Kage was responsible."

"Yes, but now we have confirmation. I don't know where he got the flute, but it was different from the others I've seen."

"How did you see this? A vision?"

"Yes. Magic came through the bond and it all played out before my eyes."

Katori paused her work.

"Magic doesn't come through the bond like that. Not that I'm aware of. Did Sion project her magic into the bond?"

"No," I replied. "She thought it was my doing."

Katori frowned and continued shoveling dirt. I forced myself onto my feet and waited for a wave of nausea to pass.

"What are you doing?"

"I'm filling in the graves."

"I see that. Why?"

Katori jabbed her shovel into the ground and ran the back of her arm across her forehead, brushing away the sweat that had collected there.

"I want to."

"Do you want some help?"

"No. This is something I must do alone."

"All right. I'm going to return to Sion. Do you

want me to bring you some water?"

"No. I'll be fine."

Katori pulled the shovel free and went back to filling in the graves. I watched her for a moment, then left her to finish the task. I walked along the street to where Sion was and found her lying in the town square. Her eyes flicked to me momentarily before she turned her attention back to a large bug that she was staring at.

I retrieved my water skin from her saddle and took a long drink. Kage was the third person to have one of those flutes. It wasn't a coincidence anymore. Someone had to be selling them, which meant that this person knew where a dragon graveyard was located. Yet another mystery without a clear path.

While I waited on Katori, I wandered around the shops near the square. It was obvious the people had fled in a hurry. Vendors had their wares still displayed, and food carts had been picked through by birds and other wildlife. As I passed by one of the vendor stalls, something shiny caught my eye. I stopped and picked it up, eyeing the item carefully. The craftsmanship was exquisite.

I wasn't sure how much the item was valued, but I decided that I needed it. Even though whoever owned the shop was probably dead, I fished a handful of coins from my pouch and set them onto the stall's counter.

"I'm buying this," I said aloud.

If the soul of the deceased person was here, then I hoped they would be pleased that I paid for it. I slipped the item into my pouch and continued my perusal of the market. By the time I'd made a complete circuit of the area, Katori had returned. She was sweaty and dirty, but she looked like she was relieved.

"Did you fill them all?" I asked.

"Yes. Now the dead can rest in peace."

I nodded and offered her my waterskin. Katori took it and drank her fill, then handed it back.

"You said Kage had one of those flutes. Can he use it whenever he wants?"

"In theory, yes. I don't know much about how they work, but I do know that they channel magic for the user. When Maren and I battled the men who used them before, they were able to use magic when Maren couldn't. They're powerful tools."

"Then we need to stop Kage before he does anything else with it."

"After we help Maren," I said.

Katori stared at me intensely. Finally, she nodded. "Very well. Let us go to her."

11

We left Taurugi behind and flew toward the coast.

The sun was slipping beyond the horizon, and darkness was slowly creeping across the landscape. I couldn't help but wonder why Kage had used such dark magic, especially since he had once been a dragon rider.

"Does Kage's dragon still live?" I shouted over my shoulder.

Katori leaned against my back and spoke near my ear.

"No. His dragon died during one of his tasks as a rider. I think that's part of what drove him away. Grief can make people do many things, even if it is a detriment to them."

She made a valid point. Still, even if he was grieving, he must have a conscience. Surely he knew that his actions were harming people other than Katori, innocent people.

Perhaps his grief has made him blind, Sion said.

Yes, I was just thinking that. It's sad that in his anguish he is tearing apart everything around him. Even his own men seemed appalled by his actions in the cemetery.

That may be something we can use against him. If those who are loyal to him don't agree with what he's doing, they will be easier to sway.

That's brilliant.

I know. Sion flooded the bond with her mirth.

I smiled and rolled my eyes.

By the time we arrived at the beach, all was dark. I spotted a lone figure next to a small fire, and we landed further down the shore to keep from flinging the sand up. As we approached, Domori was stirring something in a pot. He greeted us with a nod, his main focus on cooking. Encircled around him were green glowing souls, all watching him work.

"We're just in time for dinner," Katori said, laughing.

"So it would seem," Domori replied. "I assume there was truth to the girl's words?"

"Yes." Katori's expression darkened. "We dealt with the problem, but now we need to deal with the source."

"Kage?"

"Indeed."

I saw Demris lounging in the shadows, but I didn't see Maren anywhere. A quick scan of the water line revealed the boat wasn't here either.

"Where's Maren?" I asked.

"She said she was going to continue to ferry the souls until you and Katori got here."

That sounded like her. Always feeling the need

to be doing something. It was for a good cause, so I couldn't blame her. Still, I was excited to see her. Having to wait a little while longer was unfortunate, but all would be well.

Domori finished cooking and poured the steaming liquid into three wooden bowls that sat beside the fire. My stomach rumbled at the sight of real food.

"What is it?"

"Soup," he replied.

I grabbed one of the bowls and sat on the other side of the fire, across from Katori. I waited until the soup cooled enough, then lifted the bowl to my lips and drank a mouthful. Something solid hit my tongue, and I chewed it. It tasted good, whatever it was. I looked at Domori questioningly.

"Fish," he said, nodding toward the water.

"It's good. I don't think I've ever had this kind before."

We finished our meal and I laid against Sion, staring out at the sea. The night sky was clear, and the moon provided plenty of light. I could see the thick fog that sat atop the water in the distance, and I kept my gaze there as I waited for Maren.

I must have fallen asleep at some point. When I awoke, it was still dark. The fire continued to burn, and I saw that someone had added wood to it. I sat up and looked around. Souls flickered in and out of existence, and Katori and Domori were lying near each other, asleep by the fire. Demris made a noise, and I saw that Maren was standing near him. I hurried to my feet and walked toward her.

"Eldwin," she greeted lowly, her smile stretching across her entire face.

"I missed you."

"I missed you, too."

"When did you get back?" I asked.

"A little while ago. You looked so peaceful and I didn't want to wake you, so I tended the fire and watched you sleep."

She walked as far as she could toward me before the invisible barrier stopped her. I closed the remaining distance and embraced her tightly. The scent of her hair filled my nose, overwhelming my emotions.

"We found plenty of magical items under the school," I whispered. "Now we can start working on the bridge."

"That's great news."

"I'll wake Katori."

"No, don't. We can wait until morning. Dawn isn't far off now anyway. Come on, I want to show you something."

Maren took my hand and led me to the boat. She climbed inside and motioned for me to follow her. I hesitated, remembering the hideous mermaids that lived beneath the water's surface.

"It's all right," she said. "It's safe."

"Are you sure? I don't want to be tempted by that song again."

"We aren't going that far out."

Satisfied, I joined her in the boat and we pushed away from the shore. Maren rowed the paddles with ease, clearly having grown accustomed to handling them. She took us a few hundred feet from the shore, keeping us away from the fog, and we glided to a stop.

"So tell me, what happened since you left?"

"A lot," I replied.

I told her everything, relaying the events from when Sion and I left her behind to when Katori and I battled the undead.

"There's something I wanted to ask you. Remember when we fought the basilisk?"

"Of course."

"The magic that came through the bond and saved us at the last moment … it returned while we were in Taurugi. I had a vision that revealed everything that happened there. Kage has a dragon bone flute."

"That makes three flutes."

"I know, which tells me that someone is in the business of making them."

Maren nodded thoughtfully.

"We can let Anesko know when we return to the Citadel. He can decide if he wants to investigate it or not."

"I agree. We've dealt with enough problems lately."

"It probably sounds odd, but I've kind of enjoyed ferrying the souls to the island. I don't want to keep doing it," she added hastily when I scrunched my face. "It's just that I've had plenty of time to meet people and hear their stories. There are races of beings in our world that I've never heard of. I guess what I'm trying to say is that it's fascinating."

"That does sound fascinating," I replied. "I'm glad you were safe. I was worried about you the whole time. While Sion and I were stuck in the cavern, I thought for sure the enenra was going to kill us. Thinking about you is what kept me from giving up."

Maren smiled and leaned forward, planting a soft kiss on my lips.

"You're a good man, Eldwin."

We stared at one another in silence for a while until Maren pointed.

"This is what I wanted you to see."

I turned to look. The sun was coming up over the horizon, bathing the sky in vibrant colors. Shades of pink and orange intermingled, creating a natural work of art that was unrivaled by any painting.

"It's beautiful," I whispered.

"I know. Ferrying the souls has been great and all, but I've wanted to share this beauty with you. It reminds me of you, in a strange way."

My face flushed at her words and I blinked rapidly to keep the tears from welling in my eyes. I wanted to say something, but I wasn't sure it was the right time. The words danced at the tip of my tongue, but I kept my lips sealed. For now.

"How many trips have you made?" I asked.

"I've lost count. I'm sure it has to do with the spells on the boat, but I haven't felt tired at all. I just keep going back and forth. I don't get hungry or thirsty, either."

"That's not good. Magic or not, no one can survive without eating. Do you think we should go back now? Katori will probably be wondering where we are."

Maren stuck the paddles in the water and began guiding us back to the shore. As soon as the boat struck the sand, I climbed out and offered my hand to Maren. She clasped it and stepped out onto the shore, and together, we walked back to the fire. Katori and Domori were still asleep, but as I walked around the fire to get some food from Sion's saddle, Katori sat up.

"You're here," she said, looking at Maren.

"I am."

"Give me some time to fully wake up and we can work out how we're going to do this."

"Take your time," Maren replied. "Eat breakfast. We've got time to prepare."

Maren's perspective on this whole situation was much more upbeat than mine. I was ready to have her freed from the boat now, not when it was convenient. Domori stirred and sat up, wiping his eyes and blinking several times.

"Is it morning already?" he asked, yawning. "I'll cook something to eat."

I ate some cheese and dried biscuits, munching them down quickly, and watched Domori take his time cooking. It seemed like an eternity before Katori and Domori were fully awake and had eaten. I knew I was being impatient, but I couldn't help it.

Finally, Katori stood and retrieved one of the sacks of magical items from the pile near Demris. She opened it and pulled an item out, then looked at Maren.

"How do we unravel the spells without magic?"

12

"I've had lots of time to think about that," Maren said. "Unfortunately, I haven't come up with anything."

"Neither have I," Katori replied.

I cleared my throat. "I don't want to sound like an expert on magic or anything, but I have an idea. Even though you don't feel the magic, can you still try to cast a spell? Maybe the magic is so weak you can't feel it, but you could still use it?"

Both women stared at me with a skeptical look on their faces.

"I've tried," Maren said. "It didn't work."

"Maybe if both of you try it together?" I know I probably sounded desperate, but I refused to believe we were stuck after all we'd done to get to this point.

"We can try."

Katori held her hand out to Maren, who joined hands with her. They both closed their eyes and began whispering. After a long moment, they both sighed and opened their eyes.

"Nothing," Maren said. "The flow of magic is completely dry."

The souls around us flickered in and out of view, and I had another idea. "What if they move away. Do you think that will help?"

"It's worth a try." Maren turned to a group of souls near her. "Can you all give us some room? I promise I'll get you to the island, but we need to be able to access magic."

All at once, the souls winked out of existence. Maren closed her eyes again, her brow furrowed in concentration. Again, she sighed. She looked at me and shook her head.

"There must be something we're missing," I groaned.

"There isn't," Maren replied. "I told you, magic requires magic. Without it, we can't do much of anything."

I rubbed my hands over my face.

What about the strange magic that comes through the bond? Sion asked.

What about it?

Can you use it?

I don't know. I'm not a sorcerer, and I don't control it. It just ... happens.

Try calling on it.

I looked at Sion, wondering if she was being serious. Her giant eye blinked at me and she raised her brow expectantly.

I'll try anything at this point, I huffed.

Taking a deep breath, I placed my left hand upon Sion's snout, right between her nostrils, and closed my eyes. *Please let this work,* I prayed. Whatever this was, because I had no idea what I was doing. I sent my mind into the bond. Sion's thoughts and emotions were on the other side, swirling around me.

Wrong way, Sion's voice echoed.

Confused, I pulled back and stopped midway within the tunnel of the bond. It linked the two of us together, so I wasn't sure which "way" I should be searching. I felt along the tunnel walls with my mind, still uncertain. On the right side of the bond, near the center of the tunnel, I found a slit. It wasn't very big, and I hadn't even noticed it until I pushed my mind against the wall.

The edges were encrusted with glittering clear stones that reminded me of diamonds. They flared with light and power as I brushed against them, searing me with intense cold. I fought against the onslaught and peered into the slit. A vast power swirled just on the other side, and I immediately recognized it as the strange magic. It felt the same as it had when it flowed through the bond previsouly.

I need help! I shouted into it.

My voiceless words reverberated back at me, but the magic seemed to react. It pulsed and started moving toward the slit. I quickly fled back out of the bond, snapping my eyes open. Before I could say anything, a wave of the strange magic flooded the bond and filled my entire being. I gasped in surprise, and Maren looked at me, worry reflected in her eyes.

"What is it?" she asked.

"Give me your hand," I rasped. "Hurry!"

Sion made a rumbling noise in her throat, making my hand tremble against her scales. I kept my hand there, adding more force to ensure it stayed in place. Maren grabbed onto my mangled hand, and the magic surged through our touch. Maren's eyes widened.

"It's m-magic," she stuttered. "It's so strong!"

"Use it!" I cried.

Maren snapped her head around to look at Katori, keeping my hand in a firm grasp.

"Bring me something!"

Katori rushed forward with the item she held. It was shaped to look like an apple, but it was a large ruby. Maren took it and intoned a spell. The ruby apple flared with light. Thin cracks spread across its surface, and then the light faded and the ruby shattered into a thousand tiny shards.

Maren closed her eyes. Her lips moved but no sound came out. All of our eyes were set on her as she worked. The magic tickled my flesh as it coursed through me, but I tried to ignore the feeling. Beneath the surface of the magical flow was the same intense cold I'd felt at the slit in the bond. It was a curious thing. Maren opened her eyes and spoke a single word.

"Dispel!"

The ground trembled beneath my feet. The flames of the fire died, and a gust of wind blew across the beach, whipping the sand into a frenzy.

"Dispel!" Maren cried again.

A splintering sound filled the air, like wood breaking, and then the trembling stopped and the wind died. The boat creaked briefly before it simply fell apart.

"You did it," Katori whispered. "You unwove the spell."

A chorus of wails erupted from the souls and they flooded around us, gnashing their teeth and trying to strike us, but their incorporeal limbs and weapons passed through us harmlessly.

"Hurry, hand me another item," Maren said. "We need to start crafting the bridge before the souls start siphoning Eldwin's magic."

My magic? I ignored her comment, but only because I didn't seem to have enough focus to channel the magic into her and speak at the same time. Katori did as she asked, bringing one of the sacks over and placing it at Maren's feet. Maren pulled an item out and followed the same process, but instead of yelling the word dispel, she pointed at the edge of the shore and spoke in a language I didn't understand.

Something glimmered near the water. Maren snatched another item from the bag, unweaving the magic and using the energy to continue her work on the bridge. She went through the items swiftly and efficiently, but I could tell by the expression on her face that she was growing tired. A small portion of the bridge was visible now, but it became clear to me that this wasn't going to be a speedy process.

Ask Demris if he'll tell her that she can take a break. If the magic fades, I'll try to recall it.

There was a pause.

She's refusing. She doesn't want to risk not getting the magic to flow again.

She's as stubborn as a dragon, I said.

I'll take that as a compliment.

Her stubbornness was no match for exhaustion, however. As the minutes passed, her grasp on my hand weakened. Her arms started shaking and she slumped down onto the ground. Katori knelt beside her and peered into her eyes.

"I'll take over," she said. "You need to rest. Tell me how you're building the bridge."

Maren replied, but her voice was barely above a whisper and I couldn't make out her words. Katori nodded and stood, grabbing onto my hand. She stiffened and gave me an odd look.

"This is ancient magic."

I blinked, afraid to say anything aloud and disrupt my focus. Katori reached into the bag and picked up where Maren had left off. She worked a little slower than Maren, but she was just as efficient. Once the bag was empty, Domori brought another one over. Katori continued until she grew weary, then she switched out with Maren. And so it continued. They took turns, each allowing the other to rest so that the work remained constant.

"Do you need a break?" Maren asked me at one point.

Surprisingly, I didn't feel fatigued at all. I twitched my head to the side in an attempt to say no. She understood my gesture and kept going, but I could tell she was concerned about me. The hours passed and the bridge slowly grew, spanning over the fog and disappearing in the distance toward the island. The bags were emptied, and eventually, there was only one remaining.

"We're almost done," Maren said, matching my gaze. "We won't need to use the collar."

Her green eyes sparkled with joy, and my heart swelled with hope. She was free of the boat's enchantment, and now we were about to restore magic. The last item came out of the bag and Maren unwove the magic on it, then cast a final spell on the bridge. I expected some grandiose event, but nothing happened.

"It is finished," Maren said.

The magic flowing through the bond slowed to a trickle before fading altogether. As the last of it left my body, exhaustion replaced it and I collapsed. My muscles were like jelly and I went into a fit of coughing. Maren grabbed my waterskin from Sion's saddle and poured some of the cool liquid into my mouth.

"Thank you," I rasped.

Maren smiled at me and stood straight, turning toward the bridge.

"There is no longer a ferry to take you to the island," she called out loudly. "This bridge will now serve as the Way for the dead. Go forth and find rest!"

A multitude of souls churned around her, bowing their heads and showering her with praise. Maren smiled and exchanged words with some of the souls before they started crossing over the bridge. She knelt at my side and gave me some more water.

"Is there a safeguard to keep the souls from coming in the opposite direction?" I asked.

"No, but why would they want to come back?"

"I don't know, but it's probably a good idea to put something in place."

"He has a valid concern," Katori chimed in. "I'll craft the spell now."

She lifted her hands toward the bridge and started to speak words of power. Thunder rumbled, and a blast of lightning snaked across the sky. Something was coming across the bridge from the island. It was long and black, its form undulating as it flew through the sky. Tendrils of green smoke poured from the sides of its mouth, and as it passed overhead, I realized it was a wingless dragon. It sped across the sky, disappearing into the distance.

"What was that?" Maren asked.

Katori turned around, a look of terror on her face.

"That was the soul of Kage's dragon."

13

With the bridge completed, we returned to Katori's school.

The appearance of Kage's dragon had me worried about what he had planned, but for once, it wasn't my problem to deal with. We would take the news to Anesko and let him and the other schoolmasters decide what to do.

I just hoped he wasn't angry with us for leaving without his permission.

Sion and Demris waited in the fields outside the gates while the rest of us stood in the courtyard. Katori had asked if she and Domori could fly with us back to the Citadel to seek aid from Anesko, and we were waiting for her to finish magically locking up the school.

The flow of magic had quickly returned for the most part, but every so often, Maren would mention how there had been a sudden halt. She and Katori didn't seem concerned by that, so I assumed it was probably to be expected. Katori and Domori packed a few meager belongings and we'd strapped them to Demris's saddle. It was almost time to leave, and I decided that I couldn't wait any longer.

"Can I speak to you alone?" I asked Maren.

"Is everything all right?"

"Yes, there's just something I want to tell you."

Maren raised her brow in curiosity. I was smiling like an idiot and grabbed her hand, pulling her off to the side where no one else was within earshot. My nerves were in overdrive, but I knew that if I didn't do it now, there was no telling when the opportunity might come again.

"You know I, uh, feel strongly about you," I said.

"I do."

"And all of the things that we've been through have proven that nothing can stand between us."

"Nothing can," Maren agreed, smiling.

"While I was in the cavern with the enenra, I really thought that was going to be the end for me and Sion. I told you that it was the thought of you that kept me from giving up, and I wasn't lying. I love you, Maren. I love you more than I could ever put into words."

"I love you, too, Eldwin." Her eyes welled with tears.

I reached into my coin purse and found the item I've purchased from the market in Taurugi. Kneeling in front of her, I drew the ring out and presented it to her.

"I would be honored beyond belief if you would life-bond with me," I said. "Will you marry me?"

"You must promise me that if I become your wife, you will not try to control me."

"I will never try to control you," I swore. "I love

you for who you are and I would never want to change you."

"I know you wouldn't," she giggled, the tears falling down her cheeks. "Of course I will marry you."

"Congratulations to you both!" Katori shouted.

Maren and I laughed. I slid the ring onto her finger and it fit perfectly. I rose to my feet and turned to Katori.

"Would you be the one to bind us in marriage?"

Katori seemed taken aback. "Me? Truly?"

"Yes. You are a friend and ally, and with Maren's blessing, I would ask that it be you."

"I agree with Eldwin. Will you marry us?"

"How can I refuse?" Katori replied. "But I have one condition."

"What is it?" I asked.

"We must do it according to Terran culture."

"That's fine by me."

"Me, too," Maren said.

"Then come with me and we shall prepare you."

"Now? As in, right now?" Maren looked from Katori to me.

"Is there a reason we should wait?"

"No, there isn't," Maren replied. "Now is perfect."

"Good. Come along, then. Eldwin can help Domori with the *nage na wa.*"

"The what?"

"He will know."

Katori took Maren into the school, leaving me slightly confused. I shrugged and walked over to Domori. "Katori said that I should help you with a *nage* something?"

Domori nodded. "Yes, the *nage na wa.*"

"What is it?"

"It is something we use as a symbol in marriage ceremonies. Normally, the man will spend many days making it, but since we don't have that much time, we will make a simple design. It is less about the appearance and more about what it means."

Domori and I left the courtyard and headed into the forest that towered behind the school grounds. He instructed me to pick a couple of different flowers that I liked. While I did that, he cut a long vine down from one of the trees. I plucked as many flowers as I could carry and we returned to the courtyard.

"The vine is tied at the ends, forming a single loop," Domori said, sitting on the ground. I sat beside him and listened intently.

"It represents eternity, for that is how long a life-bond should last. The flowers ward away evil spirits, and ensure that your life-bond will be full of life and vitality."

I was amazed at how much significance something so simple could have. After Domori tied the ends of the vine, I added the flowers, spacing them out to make the most of the few I had.

"I wish I had more to put on it," I said.

"Do not worry about that. As I said, it is not what it looks like, but what it means that is important."

I nodded and we waited in silence for Katori and Maren to return. I turned my attention to the bond with Sion.

You approve of this, don't you?

If I didn't, I would have spoken already.

I'm blessed to be bonded to you.

Do you say that to all the dragons? Sion chortled.

I rolled my eyes, smiling at her humor.

Katori stepped out of the school and I rose to my feet. My heart started pounding, and my stomach churned with excitement and nervousness, a confusing mix of emotions. When Maren stepped out next, time seemed to still.

She wore a white kimono, tied across the front with a white sash. Her face had been painted white as well, with a little bit of black to accent her features. Maren looked like a being descended from the heavens, pure and holy.

Katori led her by the hand to where Domori and I were, and I moved to stand beside Maren, taking her hands in mine. Domori placed one end of the *nage na wa* around my neck and twisted it so that it was shaped like a figure eight, then placed the other end around Maren's neck.

"White embodies purity," Katori said. "Maren is pure, joining into a marriage life-bond with you. You will no longer be separate, but of one flesh. Please, recite your vows to one another."

I cleared my throat. "This is the beginning of forever, and I will honor you above all else. I will seek your guidance and love all the days of my life. I will risk everything for you and willingly lay down my life, if I must, to keep you from pain. I give you my heart. I give you my life."

Maren was no longer holding back her tears. She laughed and cried, all at the same time. I smiled at her and brushed one of the tears away. To my surprise, the paint didn't smear.

"Eldwin, you are more than I could ever have hoped for in a man. I promise to help you in every endeavor you pursue. I will dream with you, fight with and for you, and love you without measure. I give you my hand, my heart, and my life."

Katori wiped her own tears away and laid a hand on each of our shoulders.

"With these vows, you are now life-bonded. Like a pair of shears, you are joined together, often moving in different directions yet punishing whoever comes between you."

I found that to be quite a fitting analogy.

"Now kiss, and seal the bond forever."

I pulled Maren close and pressed my lips to hers, melting in her embrace. Everything faded away around us and I temporarily lost myself, forgetting all the troubles of the world. When we broke apart, I felt as if I'd awoken from a dream.

"Well, Lady Baines … what shall we do now?"

Maren smiled and squeezed my hand.

"Let's go home."

THE END OF BOOK NINE

ABOUT THE AUTHOR

Richard Fierce is a fantasy and space opera author. He's been writing since childhood, but began publishing in 2007. Since then, he's written multiple novels and short stories.

In 2000, Richard won Poet of the Year for his poem *The Darkness*. He's also one of the creative brains behind the Allatoona Book Festival, a literary event in Acworth, Georgia.

A recovering retail worker, he now works in the tech industry when he's not busy writing.

He's married and has three step-daughters (pray for him), three dogs (two huskies!), three cats, two ferrets and a fish. He basically has a zoo.

His love affair with fantasy was born in high school when a friend's mother gave him a copy of *Dragons of Spring Dawning* by Margaret Weis and Tracy Hickman.

www.ingramcontent.com/pod-product-compliance
Lightning Source LLC
Chambersburg PA
CBHW021738190726
48288CB00009B/3096